DISNEY·PIXAR
MONSTERS, INC.

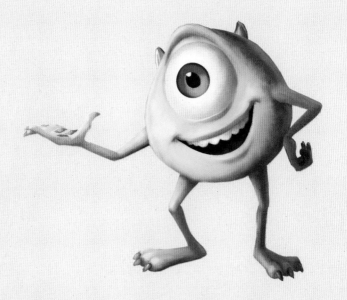

This special edition was printed for Kohl's Department Stores, Inc. (for distribution on behalf of Kohl's Cares, LLC, its wholly owned subsidiary), by Disney Press, New York/Los Angeles.

Kohl's
1224424-00
123387
09/14–10/14

Printed in China
First Edition
1 3 5 7 9 10 8 6 4 2
ISBN 978-1-4847-2383-8 • G615-7693-2-14286

For more Disney Press fun, visit www.disneybooks.com

DISNEY PRESS
New York • Los Angeles

ate one night, a little boy awoke to see . . . a monster in
his room! He screamed. Then the monster screamed.
With a sigh, the teacher turned off the mechanical boy.
Then she repeated the rules: never scream. And *never* leave a
child's door open. It could let the child into Monstropolis!

On the other side of the Monsters, Inc. building, James P. Sullivan was arriving for work. Sulley was a Scarer. It was his job to collect screams from human children. Screams were very important. Their energy powered all of Monstropolis.

Sulley was very good at his job. In fact, he and his best friend, Mike, were the best Scare Team at Monsters, Inc.

All day long, Mike set up closet doors for Sulley. And all day long, Sulley walked through the doors into children's rooms and scared them.

One evening, Mike was on his way home when Roz, the file clerk, asked for his daily paperwork. Mike had forgotten to do it!

Sulley offered to do the work for him.

When Sulley returned to the Scare Floor, he found a child's door still in its Scaring Station. Puzzled, he peeked through the door. There was no one there.

Sulley closed the door and stepped back onto the Scare Floor. Suddenly, he felt a tug on his tail.

"Kitty!" a voice called. It was a human child!

Sulley screamed. Everyone knew that human children were toxic!

He tried to return her to her room, but she wouldn't go. Finally, he hid her in a bag and went to find Mike.

Mike was at a restaurant with his girlfriend, Celia. Looking through the window, Sulley gestured for him to come outside. When they were alone, he explained what had happened. As they talked, the girl escaped and began running through the restaurant. Mike and Sulley were in big trouble!

Sulley scooped up the girl and the friends raced back to their apartment. They had to figure out a way to get her home—and fast! Mike and Sulley tried not to touch the girl. But as Mike backed away from her, he tripped and fell. The little girl giggled. The lights flashed brightly and then went out. Her laughter was even more powerful than her screams!

As Sulley put the girl to bed, he realized that she was afraid. She thought there was a monster in the closet! Sulley decided to stay with her until she fell asleep.

Later Sulley told Mike, "This might sound crazy, but I don't think that kid is dangerous!"

The next morning, Mike and Sulley dressed the girl in a monster disguise and took her to work. They had to get her to her door!

When they arrived, the office was crawling with Child Detection Agency agents. The CDA was searching for the girl. Luckily, the girl's disguise worked.

While Mike went to find the girl's door, she and Sulley played together in the locker room.

"Boo!" she said with a giggle.

Just then, Mike returned. But there was another monster close behind him. It was a Scarer named Randall. Mike and Sulley ducked into a bathroom stall. They listened in horror as Randall told his assistant to get rid of the girl.

When Randall left, Mike and Sulley snuck the girl, whom they were now calling Boo, onto the Scare Floor. But Mike had made a mistake.

"This isn't Boo's door!" Sulley said.

Just then, he realized that Boo was gone! He and Mike split up to find her.

As Mike searched the halls, Randall cornered him. He told Mike to bring her to the Scare Floor. He would have her door waiting.

Sulley found Boo playing with some little monsters. Soon Mike caught up with him. He told Sulley about Randall's plan. Together they went to the Scare Floor. But Sulley didn't trust Randall.

Determined to prove that the door was safe, Mike stepped through—and was captured by Randall.

Sulley and Boo followed Randall. They learned that he had invented a cruel new way to capture screams from kids. He was about to try it out on Mike!

Sulley rescued Mike and then raced off to find his boss, Mr. Waternoose. He needed to warn him about Randall.

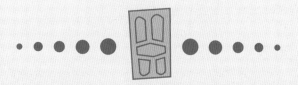

Sulley and Mike found Mr. Waternoose in the training room. They quickly explained what had happened. Mr. Waternoose promised to fix everything—but he was really working with Randall. He grabbed Boo out of Sulley's arms and then pushed the friends through an open door.

They were stranded in the Himalayan Mountains!

Sulley knew Boo was in trouble. He had to get back to
Monstropolis! He and Mike raced to the nearest village and
found a closet door to lead them home.

Sulley rushed to Randall's lab. He tore the machine apart
and saved Boo. But he still had to get her to her door!

Mike and Sulley climbed onto the machine that carried doors to the Scare Floor. "Make her laugh," Sulley told Mike. He knew Boo's laughter could power the doors.

Suddenly, Randall appeared. He chased the friends through door after door. With Boo's help, Mike and Sulley trapped Randall in a closet and shredded the door so he couldn't escape.

But they weren't safe yet! Mr. Waternoose and the CDA had taken control of the doors.

"I'll kidnap a thousand children before I let this company die!" Mr. Waternoose told Sulley.

Waternoose didn't realize that the CDA could hear him, too. He was arrested by the head of the CDA—the cranky file clerk, Roz. She had been working undercover all along!

It was time for Boo to go home. Sulley followed her into her room and tucked her into bed. He said good-bye and sadly returned to Monstropolis.

Roz ordered the CDA to shred Boo's door. No monster would ever scare her again.

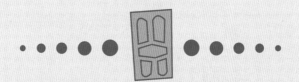

After that, the Scare Floor became the Laugh Floor. And
Sulley became president of Monsters, Inc. Sulley's discovery that
laughter was more powerful than screams meant Monstropolis
would never run out of power!

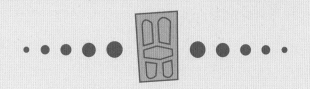

But Sulley still missed Boo.

One day, Mike told Sulley that he had a surprise. He had put Boo's door back together. Now Sulley could visit Boo whenever he wanted.

Sulley opened the door and peered inside.
"Boo?" he whispered.
"Kitty!" an excited voice replied.
The friends were reunited at last.